CIRCUS MOUSE

by LESLIE McGUIRE
illustrated by DANIEL HORNE

MERRIGOLD PRESS • NEW YORK

Text © 1986 Merrigold Press. Illustrations © 1986 by Daniel Horne.
All rights reserved. Printed in the U.S.A. No part of this book may be
reproduced or copied in any form without written permission from the
publisher. All trademarks are the property of Merrigold Press, Racine,
Wisconsin 53402. Library of Congress Catalog Card Number: 85-82188
ISBN 0-307-17706-8 MCMXCIV

Arthur was a circus mouse. He lived under the hay in Moki the Dancing Bear's cage. At least that's where he slept at night.

HOW TO BE A CLOWN

LIFE IN THE BIG TOP

During the day, there were lots of things for Arthur to do. He kept the monkeys company, polished the hubcaps on the circus wagons, and gave the lions water. Arthur even cleaned up the circus grounds after a performance. He was a hardworking mouse.

But Arthur was not a very happy mouse. He didn't want to just live with the circus. He wanted to be IN the circus.

He went to the ringmaster to apply for a job.

"Forget it!" said the ringmaster. "You're too small."

"But I could do anything," begged Arthur. "Being small doesn't matter. Just try me!"

"It wouldn't matter if you could fly through the air without a trapeze," said the ringmaster. "No one could see you. Besides, I've got troubles of my own. The clowns are sad. The juggler keeps dropping things. The elephant act is a bore. This circus is in rough shape. Sorry, kid."

Arthur felt very gloomy. He went back to his pile of hay to think. Moki tried to help.

"Why don't you go ask one of the acts for a job?" he suggested. "I hear the juggler could use some help."

So Arthur went off to see the juggler. He was dropping things left and right.

"Can you catch a wooden ball?" asked the juggler.

"Sure," answered Arthur.

Arthur almost got squashed when it landed.

"Sorry," said the juggler. "I'm afraid you're too small."

35 FT

30 FT

25 FT

20 FT

15 FT

Next Arthur went to ask the acrobats for a job. They tried him out on the human flagpole. But he couldn't hold up the flag.

"Sorry," they said. "You're too small."

Arthur decided to ask the clowns for a job. He painted his face and put on a clown suit. But the clowns didn't even notice him.

"I guess I'm just too small," said Arthur. "No one wants me for anything. But I just KNOW I can do something fantastic. I just KNOW I can."

Arthur went off to see his friend Horse. Horse was part of the trick riders act and was one of his closest friends.

THE
AMAZING
HORSE

SHOW

"No one even asks me what I can do," wept Arthur. "I mean, I can squeeze through a hole that is smaller than I am. I can climb up a table leg. I can balance on anything!"

"That's it!" shouted Horse. "You can be part of my act. You can balance on my nose!"

That night, Arthur appeared in the ring, balancing
gracefully on the tip of Horse's nose. Around and
around they went, while the trick riders did amazing
feats on Horse's back.

When the trick riders took their bows, the crowd clapped and yelled. When Horse took his bows, the crowd clapped and yelled. When Arthur took his bows, nobody clapped or yelled. "They probably couldn't see me," thought Arthur.

Then the elephants came out. Each elephant was holding on to the tail of the elephant in front of him. As they started walking around the ring, Arthur remembered what his mother had always told him.

"Stay away from elephants!" she had said. "For some reason, they are terrified of mice. They make the most awful noise and jump up and down. You might get stepped on, and then...zip... no Arthur!"

So Arthur decided to make a run for it. As he
dashed around the edge of the ring, the lead elephant
saw him.

"EEEEEEEK, A MOUSE!" he screeched.

Then the next elephant screeched,

"EEEEEEEK, A MOUSE!"

And then all the elephants started screeching,

"EEEEEEEK, A MOUSE!"

"EEEEEEEK, A MOUSE!"

And with that, they all leaped in the air.

The lead elephant landed on the stool. The next

elephant landed on the lead elephant's back. Then the rest of the elephants climbed on top of them. They made a perfect, teetering pile of groaning elephants.

The crowd whistled and clapped and hooted. They loved it.

Arthur panicked and scooted under the tent flap. He ran to his pile of hay and hid.

"Oh, my goodness," moaned Arthur. "Now I've really done it. No one will ever give me a job."

But when Moki the bear returned, he could talk of nothing but the elephants. "They were a sensation," he said. "Everyone wanted them to do the funny trick again. But they wouldn't."

"It was all my fault," sobbed Arthur. "I made them do it."

HOW TO BE A CLOWN

LIFE IN THE BIG TOP

MOKI
THE
DANCING
BEAR

"You made them do that?" cried Moki. "Go tell the ringmaster this instant. This could be your lucky break!"

BEAR'S LIFE MAGAZINE

When Arthur got to the ringmaster's tent, he was pacing up and down, muttering to himself, "This could save my circus, but how do I get them to do it again? How? I ask. How?"

"I can get them to do it," said Arthur. He told the ringmaster what had happened. The ringmaster yelled, "You've got a job, kid! This will be the greatest act in the world!"

Now Arthur has his own dressing room, and he is the star of the show.

There is a big poster that says:

ARTHUR
The Circus Mouse
The
WORLD'S
GREATEST
ELEPHANT
TRAINER